Hello, you!

Oh, please don't **look**
inside the pages
of this **book**.

Turn around and quickly run ...

The
SCHOOL
of
MONSTERS
has **begun!**

THIS BOOK
BELONGS TO

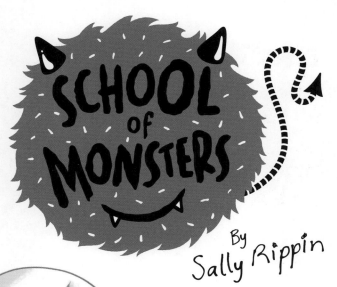

SCHOOL OF MONSTERS

By Sally Rippin

LUNA BOO

HAS FEELINGS TOO

Art by Chris Kennett

Kane Miller
A DIVISION OF EDC PUBLISHING

There are ghosts
who are scary –
and cheeky ones, too.

But others are quiet,
like dear Luna Boo.

Luna is helpful and gentle and **meek**.

PRRRRRRR^R

The best in the class
when they play hide-
and-seek.

But sometimes the monsters forget she's **around**

and finish the game
before Luna's been
found.

Oh, poor Luna Boo!
Oh, what can she do?

If you couldn't be seen, wouldn't you be mad, too?

One day when Luna's been waiting her **turn**,

she feels her head
fizzle, her cheeks
start to **burn**.

"It's MY go!" she roars. "Did you hear what I **said**?"

And to her surprise,
Luna Boo turns
bright red!

BLIP!

The monsters all
gasp, then run
far away

as Luna Boo yells,
then begs them to
stay.

Just one friend is
left, and that's
dear little Mary,

who's not scared by
things that are really
quite scary.

"I don't understand!"
Luna cries, turning
blue.

"What's happening to me? Can this really be **true**?"

But Mary says, "Oops! I just did a spell.

I can see that it's working, but maybe too **well**?

"The spell will not hurt you, it shows how you **feel,**

PIFF

PAFF

so the others can see that your feelings are **real**."

"I LOVE it!" says Luna,
and gives her a **wink**.

"But red's not my favorite. Perhaps let's try ...

"PINK!"

The next day, when Luna
is waiting her **turn**,

Dot pushes past, and Luna's cheeks **burn**.

PUSH

But now when she
opens her mouth up to
speak,

her voice comes out
clearly, not even a
squeak.

ZOOP!

She says *please* and *thank you* and mainly stays pink ...

TOOT!

except when poor William
lets out a big stink!

HOW TO USE THIS BOOK

for adults reading with children

Welcome to the School of Monsters!

Here are some tips for helping your child learn to read.

At first, your child will be happy just to listen to you read aloud. Reading to your child is a great way for them to associate books with enjoyment and love, as well as to become familiar with language. Talk to them about what is going on in the pictures and ask them questions about what they see. As you read aloud, follow the words with your finger from left to right.

Once your child has started to receive some basic reading instruction, you might like to point out the words in **bold**. Some of these will already be familiar from school. You can assist your child to decode the ones they don't know by sounding out the letters.

As your child's confidence increases, you might like to pause at each word in bold and let your child try to sound it out for themselves. They can then practice the words again using the list at the back of the book.

After some time, your child may feel ready to tackle the whole story themselves. Maybe they can make up their own monster stories, too!

Sally Rippin is one of Australia's best-selling and most-beloved children's authors. She has written over 50 books for children and young adults, and her mantel holds numerous awards for her writing. Best known for her *Billie B. Brown*, *Hey Jack!* and *Polly and Buster* series, Sally loves to write stories with heart, as well as characters that resonate with children, parents, and teachers alike.

 **HOW TO DRAW** **LUNA BOO**

① Using a pencil, start with 2 circles for eyes, eyebrows, and a small happy mouth.

② Draw 2 straight lines on either side of her face.

③ Now draw a curved line across the top and 4 bumps along the bottom.

④ Add a curly ponytail and 2 arms on the sides.

5 Draw a curved hair line. If you have one, use an eraser to remove the lines between the arms and body.

6 Time for the extra details! Add eyelashes and some rosy cheeks. Don't forget a shadow on the floor so it looks like she's floating!

Chris Kennett has been drawing ever since he could hold a pencil (or so his mom says). But professionally, Chris has been creating quirky characters for just over 20 years. He's best known for drawing weird and wonderful creatures from the *Star Wars* universe, but he also loves drawing cute and cuddly monsters – and he hopes you do too!

WELCOME
TO THE

SCHOOL
OF
MONSTERS

You shouldn't bring a pet to scho
But Mary's pet is super **cool**!

Have you read **ALL** the
School of Monsters stories?

Sam makes a mess
when he eats **jam**.
Can he fix it?
Yes, he **can**!

Today it's Sports Day
in the **sun**.
But do you think that
Pete can **run**?

Jamie Lee sure likes to **eat**! Today she has a special **treat** ...

When Bat-Boy Tim comes out to **play**, why do others run **away**?

Some monsters are short, and others are **tall**, but Frank is quite clearly the tallest of **all**!

When Will gets nervous, he lets out a **stink**. But what will all his classmates **think**?

All that Jess touches gets gooey and **sticky**. How can she solve a problem so **tricky**?

No one likes to be left **out**. This makes Luna scream and **shout**!

Now that you've learned to read along with Sally Rippin's School of Monsters, meet her other friends!

Hey Jack!

Billie B. Brown

Down-to-earth real-life stories for real-life kids!

Billie B. Brown is brave, brilliant and bold,
and she always has a creative way to save the day!

Jack has a big heart and an even bigger imagination.
He's Billie's best friend, and he'd love to be your friend, too!

Luna Boo
Has Feelings Too

First American Edition 2022
Kane Miller, A Division of EDC Publishing

Text copyright © 2021 Sally Rippin
Illustration copyright © 2021 Chris Kennett
Series design copyright © 2021 Hardie Grant Children's Publishing
First published in 2021 by Hardie Grant Children's Publishing
Ground Floor, Building 1, 658 Church Street Richmond,
Victoria 3121, Australia.

For information contact:
Kane Miller, A Division of EDC Publishing
5402 S 122nd E Ave, Tulsa, OK 74146
www.kanemiller.com
www.myubam.com

Library of Congress Control Number:
2021949075

ISBN: 978-1-68464-481-0

Printed in China through
Asia Pacific Offset

10 9 8 7 6 5 4 3 2 1